Pumpkin Soup

PUMPKIN SOUP
A DOUBLEDAY BOOK 0 385 604939

Published in Great Britain by Doubleday,
an imprint of Random House Children's Books

First published by Doubleday in 1998
This mini edition published 2002

1 3 5 7 9 10 8 6 4 2

Copyright © Helen Cooper 1998

Designed by Ian Butterworth

The right of Helen Cooper to be identified as the Author of this work has been asserted in
accordance with the Copyright, Designs and Patents Act 1988

All rights reserved. No part of this publication may be reproduced, stored in a retrieval system, or
transmitted in any form or by any means, electronic, mechanical, photocopying, recording or
otherwise, without the prior permission of the publishers.

RANDOM HOUSE CHILDREN'S BOOKS
61-63 Uxbridge Rd, London W5 5SA
A division of The Random House Group Ltd.

RANDOM HOUSE AUSTRALIA (PTY) LTD
20 Alfred Street, Milsons Point, Sydney,
New South Wales 2061, Australia

RANDOM HOUSE NEW ZEALAND LTD
18 Poland Road, Glenfield, Auckland 10, New Zealand

RANDOM HOUSE (PTY) LTD
Endulini, 5A Jubilee Road, Parktown 2193, South Africa

THE RANDOM HOUSE GROUP Limited Reg. No. 954009
www.kidsatrandomhouse.co.uk

A CIP catalogue record for this book is available from the British Library.

Printed and bound in Singapore

To
Jomai
and
Max

Pumpkin Soup

Helen Cooper

DOUBLEDAY

New York   Sydney

London   Toronto   Auckland

Deep in the woods there's an old white cabin
with pumpkins in the garden.
There's a good smell of soup,
and at night,
with luck,
you might see a bagpiping Cat through the window,
and a Squirrel with a banjo,
and a small singing Duck.

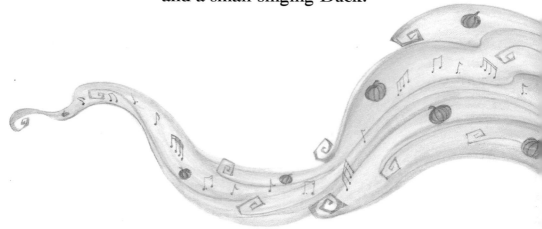

Pumpkin Soup.
The best you ever tasted.

Made by the Cat who slices up the pumpkin.

Made by the Squirrel who stirs in the water.

Made by the Duck who scoops up a pipkin of salt,
and tips in just enough.

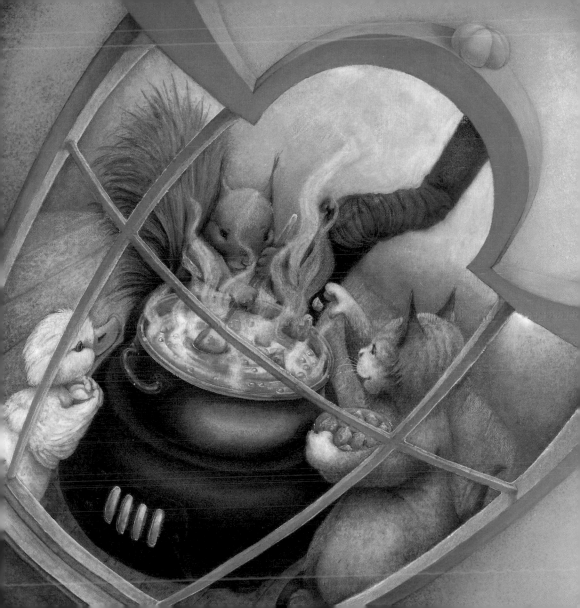

T hey slurp their soup,

and play their song,

then pop off to bed,
in a quilt stitched together by
the Cat, embroidered by
the Squirrel and filled with fine
feathers from the Duck.

And it's peaceful in the old white cabin.
Everyone has their own jobs to do.
Everyone is happy. Or so it seems . . .

But one morning the Duck
woke up early.
He tiptoed into the kitchen
and smiled at the
Squirrel's special spoon.
"Wouldn't it be fine,"
he murmured,
"if I could be the
Head Cook."

He drew up a stool,
hopped on top
and reached . . .
until his beak just touched
the tip of the spoon . . .

KER-PLONK!

Down it clattered.

Then the Duck trotted
back to the bedroom,
held up the spoon
and said,
"Today it's *my* turn to
stir the soup."

"That's mine!" squeaked the Squirrel.
"Stirring is my job. Give that back!"

"You're much too small,"
snapped the Cat.
"We'll cook the
way we always have."

But the Duck held on tight . . .
. . . until the Squirrel tugged
with all his might . . .
. . . and – WHOOPS! –
the spoon spun through
the air, and bopped
the Cat on the head.

Then there was trouble,
a horrible squabble,
a row,
a racket,
a rumpus
in the old white cabin.

TOK!

"I'm not staying here," wailed the
Duck.
"You never let me help with anything."
And he packed up a barrow,
put on his hat
and waddled away.

"You'll be back," stormed the Cat,
"after we've cleaned up."
And the Squirrel shook his spoon
in the air. But the Duck
didn't come back.

Not for breakfast.

Not even for lunch.

"I'll find him," scoffed the Cat.
"He'll be hiding outside."

"I bet he's in the pumpkin patch."

But the Duck was not in the pumpkin patch.
They could not find him anywhere.

So they waited.
All that long afternoon.

The Cat watched the door,

the Squirrel paced the floor.

"That Duck will be sorry when he comes home,"
they muttered.
But the Duck didn't come home.
Not even at soup-time.

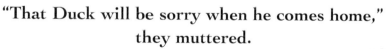

The soup wasn't tasty.
They'd made it too salty.
They didn't feel hungry anyway.
They both sobbed over supper,
and their tears dripped into the soup
and made it even saltier.

"We should have let him stir the
soup," sniffed the Squirrel.
"He was only trying to help,"
wept the Cat.
"Let's go out and look for him."

The Cat and the Squirrel were scared
as they wandered down the path,
in the dark dark woods.

They feared for the Duck all alone with the trees,
and the foxes,
and the wolves,
and the witches,
and the bears.

But they couldn't find him.

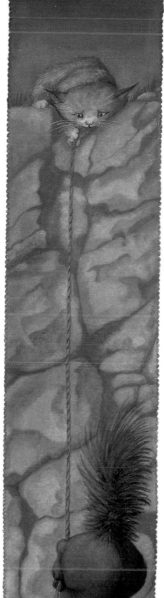

On and on
they trotted.
They reached the edge
of a steep steep cliff.

"Maybe he fell
down that!"
wailed the Cat.

"I'll save him,"
squeaked the
Squirrel,
and he scrambled
down on a long
shaky rope.
He searched
all around,
on the ground.
But he couldn't
find the Duck.

Then the Cat whispered in a sad little voice,
"Duck might have found some better friends."
"He might," yelped the Squirrel.
"Friends who let him help."

And the more they thought about it,
as they plodded back,
the more they were sure they were right.

But when they were almost home,
they saw light shining
from the old white cabin.

"It's Duck!" they shrieked,
as they burst through the door.

And Duck was *so* pleased
to see them.

He was also very hungry,
and though it was late,
they thought they
would all make . . .

...Some
Pumpkin
Soup.

W hen the Duck stirred, the Cat and the Squirrel
didn't say a word.

Not even when the Duck stirred the soup so fast
that it slopped right out of the pot.

Not even when the pot got burnt.

Then the Duck showed the Squirrel how to measure out the salt.
And the soup was still the best you ever tasted.

So once again it was peaceful
in the old white cabin.

Until the Duck said . . .

. . . "I think
I'll play the
bagpipes now."